First Printing: November 2000
Printed in Canada

9 8 7 6 5 4 3 2 1

ISBN: 09673683-3-2

Penny-Farthing Press, Inc.
P.O. Box 42043
Houston, TX 77242-2043
1-800-926-2669

Library of Congress Card Number: 00-108062

Teachers and educators:
If you would like to get more information about Mythics: The Loch series, coordinating lesson plans, or other available material for educational purposes, contact Penny-Farthing Press, toll free, at 1-800-926-2669 or go to our website at http://www.pfpress.com/lochlessons/

# PART I, FACING THE FUTURE

Created and Written by
## Marlaine Maddux

Illustrated by
## Courtney Huddleston

Inked and Embellished by
**Johnny Beware**

Colored by
**Chris Chuckry**

Penny-Farthing Press, Inc. • Houston, Texas

For Harrison,

My grandson and beloved companion
on trips to the land of stories.

# PART I, FACING THE FUTURE

Loch Ness

The Loch

# Shadows over the Loch

**F**OR THOUSANDS OF YEARS A THRIVING COMMUNITY HAS LIVED AT THE BOTTOM OF LOCH NESS, OR SHOULD WE SAY "BENEATH" THE BOTTOM OF LOCH NESS. THEY HAVE A LONG HISTORY OF OVERCOMING EVOLUTIONARY AND NATURAL THREATS. BUT NOW, THEY FACE THE GREATEST CHALLENGE TO THEIR EXISTENCE SINCE THE BEGINNING OF TIME.

"Where is Nessandra?...The Council has requested a meeting with her," explains Gran Ness.

"The Council?" Remo asks. "But why?"

"Is there danger?" Remora's voice trembles.

"There are mounting threats, Remora," Gran Ness answers. "The Council will meet and decide what must be done. Now," she presses, "do either of you know if Nessandra is at the Lava Park?"

"No Ma'am, but we'll go look for her," Remo volunteers.

# THE LAVA PARK

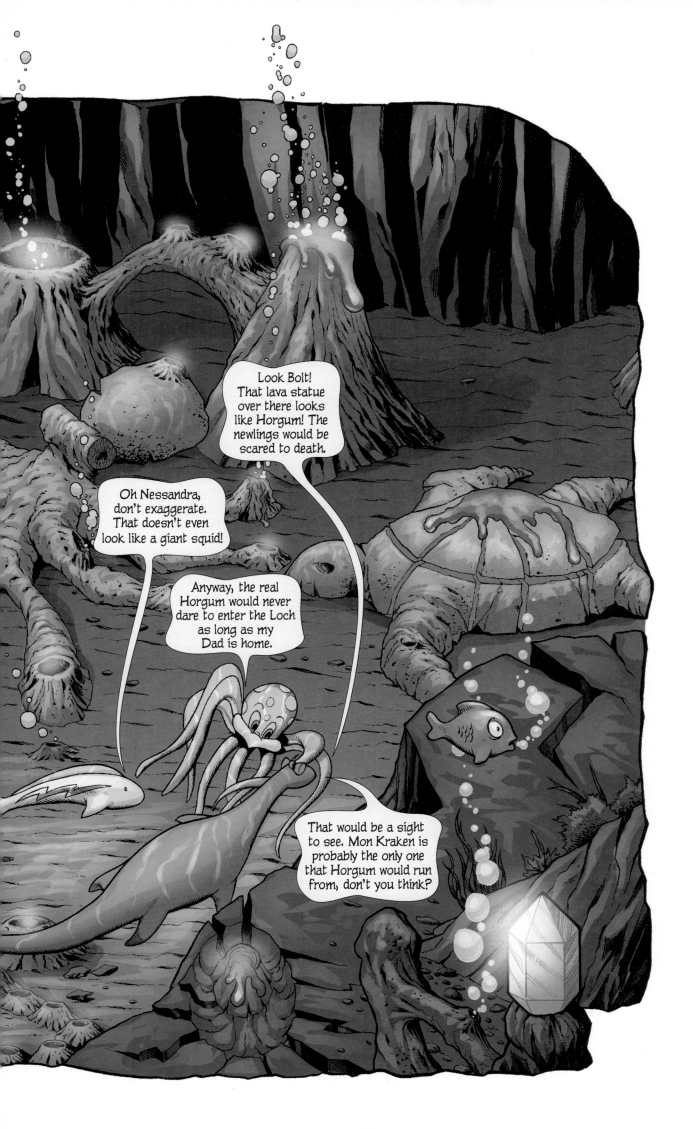

3

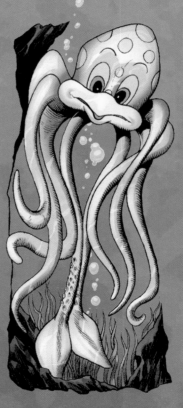

"Nessandra, Gran Ness wants you to come home," says Remo. "The Council of Ages has requested a meeting with you."

"With me?" Nessandra asks. "The Council hasn't met since the great tremor nearly three hundred years ago. Why do they want to meet with me?"

"Well, you are in line to be the next Gran Ness," answers Remo. "Haven't you thought of that?"

"My goodness, Nessandra, you'd better go," Krakey chimes in excitedly. "If the Council wants to see you, it might be about the Rite of Arcking. We'll keep looking for Allura. She's probably here, she just won't show herself."

4

"Okay! I'm going!" says Nessandra. "But find Allura and tell her that she's been selected as one of my Rite of Arcking attendants."

"C'mon, let's hurry," shouts Bolt. "I want to find Mon Zeotar and tell him I've been chosen too."

"My goodness, that's right," Krakey says, "both of our Mons will be proud that we've been honored by Nessandra."

"Let's go!" Bolt exclaims. "You can search the hiding places and I'll signal with my charges."

"Hey, what's all the shouting?" demands Allura.

"If you wouldn't disappear, you could be in on the excitement," Bolt replies.

"Don't be smart," says Allura. "What do you want?"

"You've been chosen to be one of Nessandra's attendants for the Rite of Arcking," jumps in Krakey.

"So big deal," Allura rises up. "What if I don't want to?"

"My goodness, Allura. You can't refuse. It's a big honor. In fact, the Council has requested a meeting with Nessandra," Krakey continues, "That's how important she is!"

"The Council?" Allura raises an eyebrow. "Now, that is interesting!"

# the Council of Ages

Everyone in the loch knows that the council of ages only calls a meeting when something very important must be discussed. Since the council members are the oldest and wisest inhabitants of the loch, they are smart enough to know what is important. That's why they only meet every few hundred years.

GULP!

"We present our daughter, Nessandra," Gran Ness says with pride. "Unfortunately, she is the last of our species and much hangs on her success.

"She comes before you," Gran Ness continues, "ready to accept her responsibilities and to fulfill her historical destiny as the leader of the Loch."

"Nessandra, my child, it is important that you understand your mission," Mon Torto explains. "Your Ness ancestors have always been the knowledge bringers to our world."

"You are the only ones from the Loch who can break the surface and see the other world. We know that you are preparing to perform the Rite of Arcking. However, because this is an uncertain time for the Loch, the Council has determined the need for a Knowledge Journey."

"Your grandmother, and namesake, was the last one to successfully return from the Journey," Mon Torto continues. "After the great tremor, we had to know the state of the world and the activities of the drywalkers. That was more than three hundred years ago and no other Ness since that time has been able to accomplish the Journey. Nessandra, a great responsibility now falls on your shoulders," Mon Torto says kindly. "It is important for us to see again, and you can give us eyes to a world we must always watch. Do you understand?"

"Yes, sir."

All eyes turn toward Gran Pucashark as she moves forward. "The drywalkers are an aggressively curious race, and in recent times they have been descending deeper and deeper toward our community."

"They have new devices that are like closed shells with windows. Your mother has seen them attempt to lower themselves in these shells. The muddy waters above us have kept us hidden, but we must know how far their science can take them."

"In the past, many objects from the surface have penetrated the world's waters and now rest on the ocean floors. These hand crafted objects have taught us much about this species and revealed to us how they have progressed over the centuries," Gran Pucashark's voice is serious. "It has been many years since your grandmother returned from her Knowledge Journey around the world. We expect you to discover new evidence of the drywalker's progress. Do you understand?"

"Yes, ma'am."

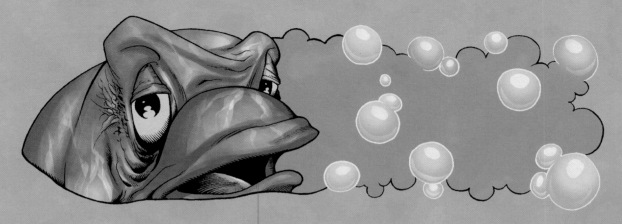

Mon Coelacanth leans forward and focuses his wise eyes on Nessandra. "My Coelacanth brothers and sisters, as well as The Council of Ages, believe we are facing a threatening period in our history."

"My species has lived for 80 million years and we have witnessed every major upheaval and renewal since that time. For hundreds of centuries we have patiently attempted to understand the world above us. During this time the drywalkers have caused little interference."

"However, they now appear to be in a time of unprecedented advancement and may come in large numbers to explore our realm." Mon Coelacanth lowers his kind voice, "Nessandra, your unique species is threatened with extinction. You are the last in a line of knowledge gatherers. This Knowledge Journey may be our final opportunity to glimpse the future for the Loch. Do you understand?"

"Yes, sir."

"And remember, Nessandra," Mon Lipilung rises up, "besides knowledge, there is another form of light you must bring to the Loch."

"The light crystals which illuminate our deep world must be replenished."

"You will travel to Atlantis and return with our precious energy source," Mon Lipilung's voice softens, "Do you understand?"

"Yes, sir."

# Afterwards...

"Don't be sad, young one," Mon Ness assures Nessandra, "It is a great and honorable privilege to go on the Knowledge Journey. You know you can name three young companions to accompany you on the trip. They should all possess abilities that will contribute to the success of your mission. Perhaps you will name the ones you've previously chosen to be your Rite of Arcking attendants."

Nessandra looks up at her father, "Yes, sir."

Mon Ness smiles affectionately at his daughter, "Of course, the Rite of Arcking ceremony must wait until you return from your journey. Then it will be an even greater time of rejoicing. Nessandra, very few of our kind have been selected to perform this service and even fewer have returned. You will encounter many perils in the outside world, but if you are successful, you will return older and wiser and you will still have over two hundred years to live as the leader of the Loch."

"Yes, my darling," Gran Ness agrees. "You will be the leader in a time of change for our world and if you are able to return from the journey, you may become one the most honored plesiosaurs to ever live."

"Now, my dear," Gran Ness continues, "are you ready for your father and I to help you prepare for your departure?"

Yes, Mother.

3

the
Time
Approaches

It's been long understood that the tradition of the knowledge journey is a necessary link with the outside. However, while it is always cause for great excitement in the loch, the citizens of the community realize that coming face to face with the unknown requires the bravery of each member of their isolated world.

Especially aware of the courage shown by the chosen few who successfully return from the hazardous journey, these heroes are always honored with a monument.

# PLESIOSAUR POINT
## *Valley of Heroes*

To prepare for her trip, Nessandra turns to the one plesiosaur who can help her - her grandmother. She is excited about studying her grandmother's writings. They had been stored in the Loch Archives for hundreds of years and read only by her parents and members of the Council. She feels sure that those writings will hold the secret to a successful Knowledge Journey and help boost her confidence about leaving the Loch.

# THE LOCH ARCHIVES

When you exit the Neptune Tunnel, you will be far out into Mer Madre in a place called *The Bermuda Triangle*. The Bermuda Basin Dolphin League will help you prepare for your journey by teaching you to discover the knowledge you already have inside yourself. It is an ability to recognize the truth and not be misled by false images known as *bogussos*. After this preparation, your next stop will be *The Desoto Canyon*, which contains the tunnel entrance for your transit to *Mer Padre*, the larger deep water ocean beyond the western continental barrier.

## AT HOME

Remo sees the serious look on Nessandra's face. "Don't worry about Spiny. We'll take care of him for you. He'll be just fine."

"Yes, dear," Remora tries to sound reassuring, "I'll feed him cuddlecrop every day."

Nessandra forces a little smile, "Thank you. I'll miss him."

"I don't mean to interrupt your studying, Nessandra," Gran Ness says from the doorway, "but I've prepared some feather frond for you to take on your trip. I know there will be times when eating a bit of this will remind you of the Loch and comfort you."

"Thank you, Mother," Nessandra says gratefully.

"Remo, Remora, could you please leave us alone for a few moments?" Gran Ness requests.

"Yes, ma'am," they answer together.

Gran Ness speaks softly to Nessandra, "Child, the Knowledge Journey is long and difficult. I want you to know that if you ever have moments of despair, you may use the Link. It is a sacred ability and demands much energy."

"Yes, I understand. I only have a memory of using it that one time."

"I remember dear. You were small and Horgum frightened you with his threats against the Loch. You used the Link well and we sent Mon Kraken to drive him off," Gran Ness pauses. "Just remember, Nessandra, that it is within you if you need to communicate with us."

"Mother," Nessandra hesitates, "there's something I've been wanting to ask you. I know I'm old enough to have a tulip tail. Why hasn't it happened?"

"Oh, my darling. I had no idea you were thinking of that. I'm so sorry," Gran Ness's voice is sad. "You have to fall in love...before the tulip tail grows."

## ... Later

"Father, when you were little, did Grandmother tell you about her Knowledge Journey?" Nessandra eagerly asks.

"When I was old enough to understand, Gran Mama Ness would tell me stories about wonderful and strange places," Mon Ness answers. "Some of the same stories I've told you. She was especially fond of Atlantis and the crystal traders."

"No... I mean, Father, did she tell you how it changed her? How it made her feel about the Loch?" Nessandra insists.

"Why yes, young one, she did speak of it," Mon Ness looks down at Nessandra. "That is a wise question. She told me that learning about others was really learning about herself."

"Huh?"

"It's not something I can tell you. It's something you must experience for yourself... and you will."

"Father," Nessandra smiles, "I've always been proud to have Grandmother's name, but I was a baby when she crossed to Drumvalla. Lately, though, like when I was studying her writings in the Loch Archives, I had the strangest feeling that she was close by."

24

# The Krakens

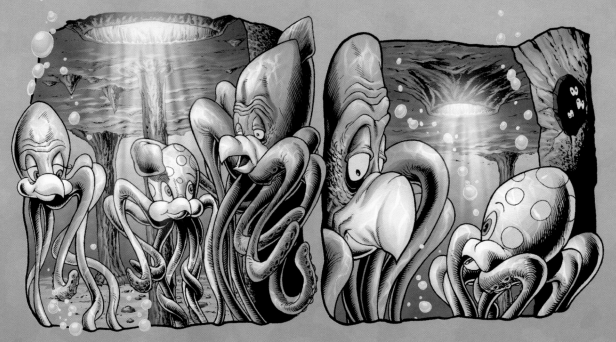

"Son," Mon Kraken says in his deep voice, "you and Nessandra have been friends since you were small, but now she is the leader of the Knowledge Journey and you must use your Kraken abilities to help her succeed in her mission."

"Yes, sir, I will...but sir," Krakey hesitates, "I worry that my arms are not long enough and powerful like yours."

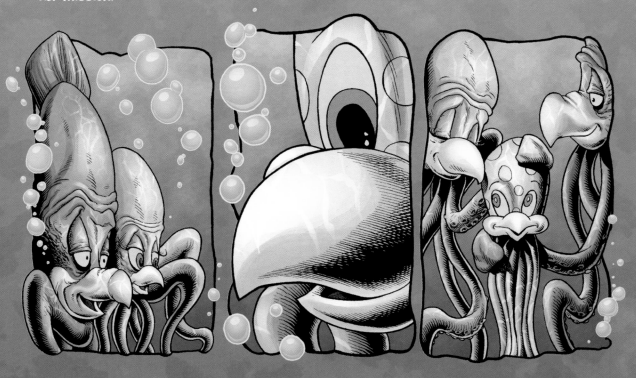

Mon Kraken smiles. "Do not concern yourself, son. You will soon be as large as I, perhaps larger."

"And remember, Krakey," his mother adds, "you can still use your arms to search the places that the others can't reach. ...and what about the ink you can shoot for everyone to hide in?"

"Don't forget, Krakey," Mon Kraken reminds his son, "your most fearsome weapon is your strong beak. Because you can crush anything you choose, your true power lies in wisely knowing when the time is right."

"I...I think I'm ready," Krakey looks up at his parents.

# The Zeotars

"Bolt, I'm sorry that I haven't been around more," says Mon Zeotar. "I didn't even notice how fast you can swim or that your charges are growing stronger. I also regret that your mother isn't alive to see you receive this honor. If she were here, I know she would be proud."

"Dad, Dad, watch this!"

"BOLT! STOP! Learn to control yourself! You can't wildly throw charges without first developing accuracy. ...This is when I really miss your mother."

"I'm sorry, Dad," Bolt apologizes.

"Look son," Mon Zeotar says more gently, "maybe I haven't been very good at teaching you discipline and responsibility. You've been chosen to go on the Knowledge Journey and everyone will be depending on you for your speed and your charges. You need to be ready. Come, let's go practice."

# Allura

"I should have stayed invisible.  The Loch is the only home I know and I don't like being told that I have to go outside on some silly journey.  I don't remember much about my early years anyway, except that the world was cold and miserable when Mon Torto found me struggling in the Neptune Tunnel and brought me to the Loch."

"But, on the other hand," Allura thinks to herself, "except for the Tortos, I don't have any family here.  ...For that matter, I don't have any family anywhere."

"Oh well, who knows," she muses.  "It might be different.  I was getting bored around here anyway.  Maybe I can play some tricks and have a little fun with that gang of goofy gills."

"Hi, Gran Mama. Tomorrow we leave the Loch and I'm a little bit afraid. I wish I could link with you, but there are no links with Drumvalla. Gran Pucashark and Mon Torto tell me that I am like you. That makes me feel better. I hope they are right, but I'm not sure I'm as brave as you were or smart enough to learn about bogussos from the Bermuda Basin Dolphin League. Anyway, Gran Mama, I know you will be watching me tomorrow and that will give me courage to lead my friends into the Neptune Tunnel."

4

# Leaving the Loch

EVERYONE IN THE LOCH KNOWS WHERE THE PASSAGE TO THE NEPTUNE TUNNEL IS LOCATED. IT HAS THE PLESIOSAUR SYMBOL ABOVE THE OPENING. HOWEVER, NO ONE WOULD DARE ENTER THIS SACRED PORTAL, FOR IT IS THE DANGEROUS ROUTE TO MER MADRE AND THE OUTSIDE WORLD. ONLY THE PLESIOSAURS AND OTHERS DESIGNATED BY THE COUNCIL OF AGES WOULD ATTEMPT TO TRAVEL THIS TREACHEROUS PATH.

"Remember, Nessandra," Mon Ness reminds, "the current is very strong in the Neptune Tunnel. You must relax and let it carry you. Also remember, before you can reach Mer Madre, you will have to request assistance and permission from Gran Morag Morar."

"Don't let her frighten you," Gran Ness speaks up. "She can be quite grumpy when travelers disturb her. But if you are respectful and polite, she will help you. Remember, you must speak in rhyme or she will not listen." Gran Ness's face softens into a smile, "Farewell, Darling. We will yearn for your safe return."

"Your sensing ability will be valuable on this journey," Mon Torto advises Allura. "You can help them avoid possible trouble. Also, in case there is a need for it," he continues, "remember all the medical remedies that Gran Torto taught you. Nessandra will look to you for advice on these matters." Mon Torto's kind voice hesitates, "Allura, my child, it is probably best that you visit the world outside again. You have much memory to regain and it is time."

"Krakey," his mother assures him, "when you are frightened or worried, remember that you are the son of Mon Kraken. You are destined to follow his legend and become the largest and most feared giant squid in the oceans."

"My goodness, Mom," Krakey replies, "I wish you wouldn't remind me."

"Bolt," Mon Zeotar impresses on his son, "stay focused, work with your friends, and listen to Nessandra." He pauses. "If you will harness your power and use your strengths wisely, you can proudly carry the name of Zeotar. Good luck, son!"

# Time to go...

Goodbye! Goodbye!

"Who wants to go first?" asks Nessandra.

"My goodness, w-w-why can't we all jump together?" Krakey's voice trembles.

"What a bunch of babies!" Allura shouts.

"Oh yeah? I don't see you jumping," Bolt retorts.

"Okay, stop!" Nessandra orders. "Krakey had a good idea. When I count to three, we will ALL jump. ONE...TWO..."

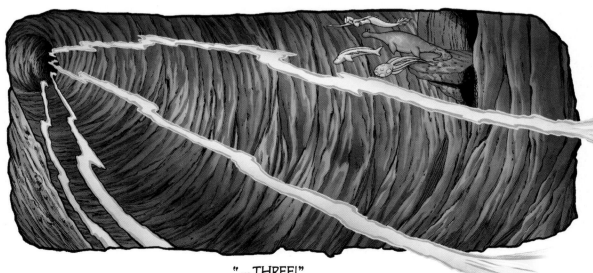

"...THREE!"

"BONDOLAY!!" Bolt suddenly screams.

On their way...

"WHEEEEE!"

"Bolt, why did you scream BONDOLAY?"
Nessandra asks. "You know that shout is
part of the Rite of Arcking."

"I don't know," Bolt answers sheepishly.
"It just felt like the right thing to say."

"Look," Nessandra cries, "There's
Morag's portal!"

"Where is Morag?" Nessandra wonders.
"I thought she was supposed to be guarding
the entrance."

"My goodness," Krakey worries, "I hope she
won't be angry that we're entering."

"Oh, don't be such a baby," Allura pipes up.
"What's she going to do?"

"UH OH!"

"RROAAAAAARR!"

"WHO SAID YOU COULD CALL
AT MY DOOR IN THE WALL?"

Nessandra steps forward.

"Please show us the way Gran Morag Morar.
The portals are many, Mer Madre's so far.
"We ask for your mercy to shine on us four.
We ask for your beacon to light the right door."

"My Loch is not open for all eyes to see.
Why should I help you without any fee?"

Nessandra replies,
"My mother, Gran Ness, respectfully asks,
consider our problem and help with our task."

"Ah, you are Nessandra,
Loch leader to be.
Why didn't you say?
'Tis a pleasure for me."

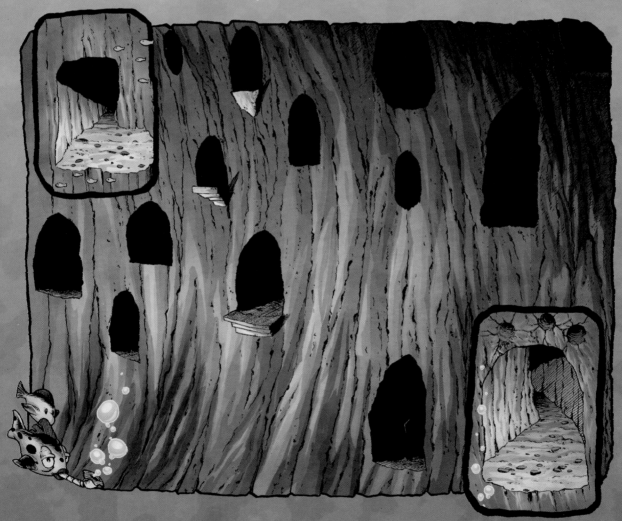

"So listen real hard, I'll give you the route.
You'll come to a portal that looks like a boot.

This path will take you to Nineteen Door Bay.
Then look for the symbol to show you the way.

At the top of the door, three circles will show.
This is your sign and the way you must go."

"Stay in the shaft till the walls open wide.
This is Mer Madre, I'm now not your guide."

5

# the Bermuda Triangle

ENTERING THE QUIET VASTNESS OF MER MADRE, THE FOUR TRAVELERS ARE MOMENTARILY SPEECHLESS. THE ENORMITY OF THEIR MISSION IS SUDDENLY QUITE CLEAR AND EACH ONE OF THEM IS FILLED WITH INNER DOUBT. HOWEVER, DETERMINED TO OBEY THE DIRECTIONS OF GRAN MAMA NESS'S WRITINGS, THEY ARE HEADING TO THE SOUTHWEST AND GRAN MAMA'S SECRET TUNNEL IN THE DESOTO CANYON. THIS LONG PASSAGE IS SUPPOSED TO CARRY THEM TO THE STRANGE OCEAN CALLED MER PADRE ON THE OTHER SIDE OF THE WORLD. BUT FIRST, THEY MUST PASS THROUGH A DANGEROUS AREA OF MER MADRE KNOWN AS THE BERMUDA TRIANGLE. UPON ENTERING THESE WATERS, THEY ARE TO CONTACT THE BERMUDA BASIN DOLPHIN LEAGUE. IT IS FROM THEM THEY WILL LEARN HOW NOT TO MISTAKE FALSE IMAGES OR WRONG THINKING, CALLED BOGUSSOS, FOR WHAT'S REAL.

Swimming out of the protection of the Neptune Tunnel, Allura has begun to sense a disturbing higher frequency in the water.

"I feel something. It's pulling me to the west."

"Is it the dolphins?" asks Nessandra.

"No, no," Allura responds. "It's not alive."

"Wh...what do you mean, Allura?" Krakey stutters.

"Don't worry, Krakey," Nessandra assures, "Allura doesn't sound afraid. Let's go find out what it is."

"That's it!" Allura gasps. "That's what I sensed."

"What is it?" Nessandra asks.

"Maybe it's not really there, maybe we're seeing a bogusso," Krakey's voice trembles.

"Don't be silly," Nessandra says impatiently. "It must be part of a drywalker's wooden ship."

"Oh good! My charges can burn holes in wood. Let me see!" shouts Bolt.

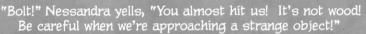

"Bolt!" Nessandra yells, "You almost hit us! It's not wood! Be careful when we're approaching a strange object!"

Behind them, Allura's voice quivers with emotion, "There is sadness here...great loss."

Before Allura can say more, a loud shout of greeting comes toward them.

"YO HO! YOU ARE HERE! We've been waiting for you," announces the visitor. "The eleven Masters of the League have come together to show you the images of truth."

"What? Who are you? And how did you know to expect us?" asks Nessandra.

"The Masters see everyone who enters or leaves the Triangle. Nesses have been enlightened by the League since the very first Knowledge Journey," the stranger answers. "I'm your dolphin guide. Come! Follow me!"

"Welcome travelers!" says the Master leader. "You have finally arrived. Do you know why the Triangle waters are the first stop on your journey?"

"To learn how not to be fooled when we are looking at a bogusso?" Nessandra answers.

"Yes, that's right," says the leader. "This part of Mer Madre is full of illusions and it's easy to be misled. If you learn how to listen to yourself and what you know to be true, you will be less afraid while you explore the deep ocean on your journey." He pauses, "It will not be easy.

"We know you have already encountered an object on the ocean floor. Perhaps that would be a good example to start teaching you about bogusso illusions. You can see it projected above.

"Now, let us begin showing you the other images while you ask any questions you might have."

"No, the sadness you felt was true, but it is good that you are questioning what you saw.

"The world outside the Loch doesn't feel safe. It's harsh and strange to me. I don't think I like it. The object we found was full of pain. Was that a bogusso?"

One of the lessons of a bogusso illusion is to not always trust your eyes. The piece of wreckage you found was from a drywalker airship that was on its own Knowledge Journey."

"WOW! Was it exploring the Triangle?" Bolt asks excitedly.

"No, the airship was on a journey to worlds far above our realm."

"There was a disaster and the flight ended in tragedy. Pieces of their ship fell back into the water and ended up on our ocean floor."

"Oh, no! Did a bogusso cause them to make a mistake?" an alarmed Nessandra asks. "Knowledge Journeys are too dangerous. What if I won't be able to recognize bogussos and we fail, just like the drywalkers did?"

"No, no my dear, you must not think that way," the Dolphin Master assures her. "Failures occur when we don't recognize a true hazard for what it is. Some see hazards that don't exist, while others fail to see the real risks." He pauses. "True failures only occur when there is no learning. The drywalkers learned many important truths from that journey."

"M...My goodness," says Krakey, "you would have to be very brave to face a bogusso. Maybe it would be better if we all returned to the Loch."

"That's not the answer, son," the Dolphin Master patiently replies. "Someday you must learn how seeing a bogusso can trick you into wrong thinking. If you do it now, everyone will be proud of you ...but more important, you will be proud of yourself."

"But I'm still not sure I would know a bogusso," Krakey shivers. "The drywalkers didn't see the illusion they faced and look what happened!"

"That's true. While traveling through our waters, many drywalkers have lost their way," the Dolphin Master continues, "but that is because when they see a bogusso illusion, they won't slow down and look carefully at the truth. Other times, fear keeps them from sensing what's right."

"This happens to all of us sometimes. Because our minds are not clear or we are anxious to believe something, we do not stop and question what we see - even when we have a funny feeling.

"So remember, if something doesn't look or feel quite right," the Dolphin Master continues, "you can often see better when you close your eyes and listen. Then...the stillness within you unlocks the truth."

"You mean that I'm smarter than a bogusso?" asks Nessandra. "You can be...you all could be... if you would learn to trust yourselves," the Dolphin Master answers.

"But that sounds simple," replies Allura impatiently.

"Yes, perhaps finding the truth IS simple...but recognizing it is not." He pauses to let the meaning sink in. "If you practice asking yourself the truth, you will soon recognize it quickly. Now we must go...don't forget what we have told you."

## SAYING GOODBYE...

"We have shown you all we can," their friendly dolphin guide calls after them. "The rest is up to you. Getting to the Desoto Canyon is dangerous. You must travel in shallow water on your way and the drywalkers frequently explore this area. Beware and be wise."

## "YO HO, MY FRIENDS!"

THE KNOWLEDGE JOURNEY IS UNDERWAY! NESSANDRA, KRAKEY, BOLT, AND ALLURA ARE FILLED WITH A MIXTURE OF EXCITEMENT AND FEAR. WHAT LIES AHEAD OF THEM WILL TEST THE LIMITS OF THEIR STRENGTH, INTELLIGENCE, AND MATURITY.

THEY WILL ENCOUNTER CHALLENGES FROM THE VERY FIRST CHAPTER OF PART II WHEN THEY VISIT THE DESOTO CANYON AND ARE PRESENTED WITH A CHANGE OF PLANS. TRAVELING AROUND THE TIP OF SOUTH AMERICA AND THROUGH THE DRAKE PASSAGE WILL LEAD THEM TO A MEETING WITH AN UNFORGETTABLE CHARACTER NAMED OLD MON LOUIE. THEY BECOME WORRIED AND ON THE LOOKOUT FOR BOGUSSOS WHEN THEY ARE WARNED NOT TO VENTURE TOO CLOSE TO THE DANGEROUS AND LEGENDARY GREAT BARRIER REEF. AS OUR CHARACTERS MOVE NORTH, A GRIEVING FAMILY OF HUMPBACK WHALES INVOLVES THEM IN THEIR STORY. TRAVELING TO THE WATERS OFF THE COAST OF BAJA, MEXICO, THEY ARE CAUGHT UP IN AN ADVENTURE WITH ONE OF THE RAREST CREATURES TO EVER EXIST, THE CADBOROSAURUS. IT IS THIS ENCOUNTER THAT POINTS THEM TOWARD PART III AND THE ANSWER TO A LONGSTANDING MYSTERY AMONG THE INHABITANTS OF THE LOCH.

AS OUR STORY PROGRESSES FURTHER INTO PART III, EACH CHARACTER IS FORCED TO FACE THE PROBLEMS AND JOYS OF GROWING UP AND REALIZING WHAT IT IS THAT WILL ULTIMATELY SHAPE EACH ONE OF THEM INTO THE ADULTS THEY ARE MEANT TO BE. ALL OF THEM KNOW THAT THEY WILL BE EXPECTED TO STEP INTO THEIR RIGHTFUL PLACE AS A CITIZEN OF THE LOCH.

## ASSUMING, THAT IS, THEY ALL RETURN SAFELY HOME...

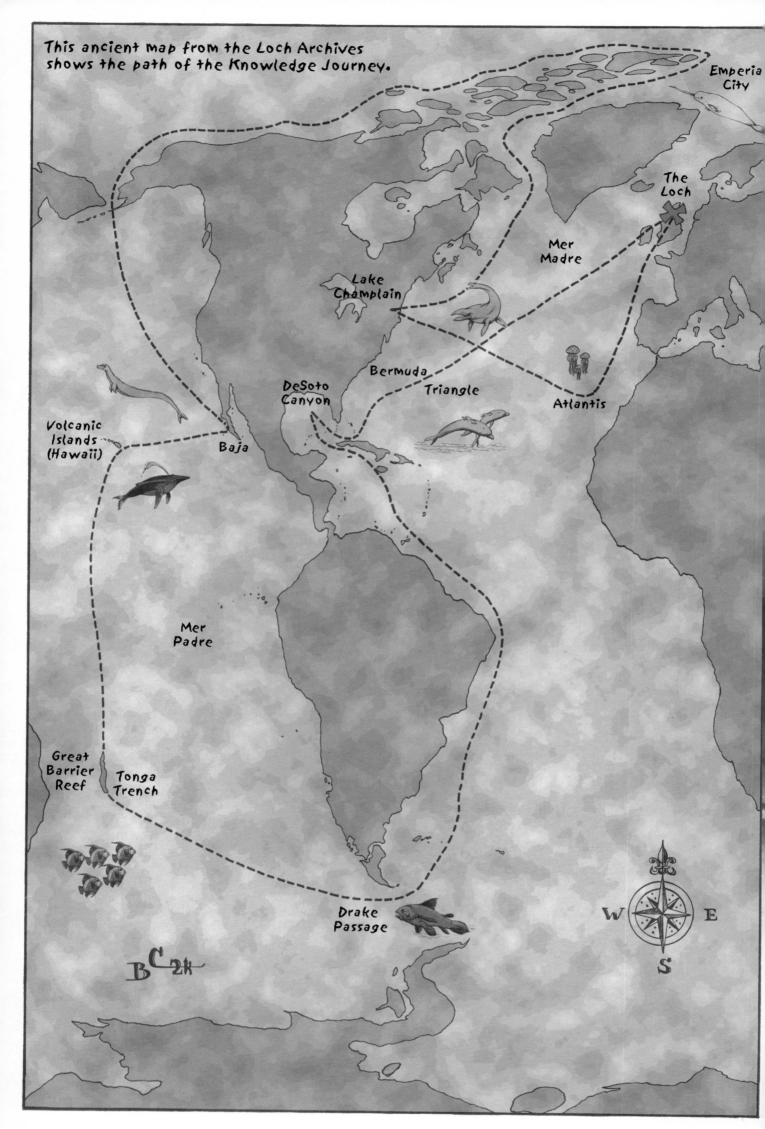

This ancient map from the Loch Archives
shows the path of the Knowledge Journey.

Emperia
City

The
Loch

Mer
Madre

Lake
Champlain

Bermuda
Triangle

Atlantis

DeSoto
Canyon

Volcanic
Islands
(Hawaii)

Baja

Mer
Padre

Great
Barrier
Reef

Tonga
Trench

Drake
Passage

W

E

S

B C 2K

50

# The Loch Lexicon

## PART I

### A Glossary for Drywalkers

**Atlantis** – Far from the safety of the Loch, Atlantis is the legendary sunken island where our travelers must bargain for the precious light crystals that will keep the Loch inhabitants from the darkness.

**Bermuda Triangle** – A large and dangerous area of Mer Madre located off the southeastern coast of the United States. Known among the Loch creatures for its many mirages, the tips of the triangle that make up this area of illusion are Bermuda, Miami, Florida, and San Juan, Puerto Rico.

**Bermuda Basin Dolphin League** – A troop of dolphins that aid travelers moving through their waters. The **MASTERS OF THE LEAGUE** are the eleven dolphins who lead the league and show visitors how to distinguish between a bogusso and what's real.

**Bogusso (bo-goose-oh)** – An illusion or mistake about what is believed to be true. The ability to tell the difference between what is a bogusso and what is real is a very important part of Nessandra's Knowledge Journey.

**Council of Ages** – Legendary panel made up of the oldest and wisest creatures that live in the Loch. Their knowledge and experience earns them great respect among the Loch inhabitants. They are always consulted in times of crisis and need.

**Desoto Canyon** – Underwater canyon southeast of Pensacola, Florida, distinguished by colder water temperatures. According to Gran Mama Ness's directions, the 6,000-foot deep canyon contains the tunnel entrance leading to Mer Padre.

**Drumvalla (drum-va-la)** – For the creatures of the Loch, Drumvalla is heaven or paradise.

**Drywalkers** – What the inhabitants of the Loch call humans.

**Gran** – A title of respect for the female elders of the Loch.

**Gran Mama Ness** – Nessandra's grandmother and the last plesiosaur to take the historic Knowledge Journey. It is through her writings that Nessandra is guided on her quest throughout the world's oceans.

**Gran Morag of Morar (gran more-rag of moor-ar)** – South of Loch Ness, Morag is the plesiosaur ruler of Loch Morar and guardian of the nineteen portals that lead out of the Neptune Tunnel. Only responsive to speech that rhymes, she is the one who grants permission and assistance to travelers who wish to use her portals.

**Gran Pucashark (gran poo-ca-shark)** – Oldest of all her shark cousins, Gran Pucashark is a member of the respected Pucapampella (poo-ca-pam-pell-a) species. With a family tree that goes back over 400 million years, she has seen and heard about the many changes the world has gone through, and therefore knows the time for change is once again at hand.

**Horgum** – A roaming giant squid with a bad attitude, Horgum is an unwelcome visitor to the Loch and its inhabitants. Happiest when scaring newlings and creatures much smaller than he, nobody likes it when Horgum is seen slithering around the depths of their realm.

**Knowledge Journey** – Led by a member of the Ness family, the Knowledge Journey is a search by creatures of the Loch for information and truths about the world outside their protected realm.

**Link, (the)** – A psychic method of communication that only Nessandra and her family possess. Linking is physically exhausting, so Nessandra only uses this power when absolutely necessary.

**Loch (the)** – Located beneath Loch Ness, the Loch is the protected home of hundreds of animal species. Most of the Loch's inhabitants prefer to stay within its boundaries. However, some creatures have been known to venture outside to try and get a peek at the strange, air-breathing creatures known as drywalkers.

**Loch Ness** – Located in Scotland, Loch Ness is thought by drywalkers to be about 132 meters deep—that's about 433 feet! Because of its muddy waters though, they can't be very sure where the water ends and the bottom of Loch Ness begins.

**Mer Madre (mare ma-dray)** – Known to drywalkers as the Atlantic Ocean.

**Mer Padre (mare pa-dray)** – Known to drywalkers as the Pacific Ocean.

**Mon** – A title of respect for the male elders of the Loch.

**Mon Coelacanth (mon see-la-canth)** — As wise as he is ancient, Mon Coelacanth is a member of the oldest family of fish on Earth. Accomplished and experienced, he has a lot of knowledge to offer Nessandra for her voyage.

**Mon Kraken (mon cray-ken)** — Father of Krakey, he's the largest and most respected giant squid in the ocean. Often called upon to protect the Loch and its inhabitants from Horgum, he is known throughout the sea as a guardian and protector.

**Mon Lipilung (mon lip-ee-lung)** — Sitting on the Council of Ages, Mon Lipilung is from one of the oldest families of lungfish — the Lepidosiren (lep-id-o-sy-ren). His ancestors have survived throughout history, through floods and droughts, good times and bad. This heritage has shown Mon Lipilung how to endure when the world around him changes.

**Mon Torto (mon tor-toe)** — Hundreds of years old, Mon Torto is the oldest turtle in the Loch and maybe the world. Finding Allura when she was a newling, he raised her as his own.

**Mon Zeotar (mon zee-o-tar)** — Father of Bolt, Mon Zeotar has raised Bolt alone since the death of Bolt's mother. A member of the ancient lightning fish family (only found in the Loch and never before seen by the outside world). With his strong tail fin and slick body, Mon Zeotar is one of the fastest fish in the sea and can throw his charges with incredible accuracy and distance.

**Neptune Tunnel** — An undersea Tunnel leading from the Loch to Mer Madre. Swift currents make it very dangerous, but it's the only underground path out of the Loch.

**Newlings** — The baby creatures of the Loch.

**Plesiosaur (pleez-ee-o-soar)** — Roaming the oceans during
the late Triassic period (about 213 million years ago) to the
Cretaceous period, plesiosaurs are thought to have become extinct
nearly 65 million years ago.  Nessandra and her parents, being members
of the plesiosaur family, would beg to differ with these
drywalker findings.

**Portal (poor-tall)** — A gateway or door.

**Rite of Arcking** — The Rite of Arcking is a ceremony in
which a young Ness breaks the surface of the water of Loch
Ness for the first time.  This ritual is the beginning step in the
preparation toward being named the new leader of the Loch.

**Shaft** — A long narrow passage.

**Tulip Tail** — A trait passed on from generation to generation in Nessandra's family.  When
the females of her kind fall in love, a tulip shaped feature develops on the tip of their tails.  This
growth is called a tulip tail.

# OLD MON LOUIE INVITES YOU TO JOIN HIM IN PART II OF
# THE LOCH
## "THE KNOWLEDGE JOURNEY"

I say, I say,
I welcome you to
visit me soon.
I promise it will be
an adventure.
Right-o,
an adventure,
right-o.